Veterans
HEROES IN OUR NEIGHBORHOOD

By **Valerie Pfundstein**
Illustrated by **Aaron Anderson**

Pfun-omenal
Stories

Dedication

With heartfelt gratitude to all the men and women who serve our country, and in loving memory of the first veteran I knew—my grandfather, Frank Falotico (1908–1983).

—V. P.

To Eric, Mike, and Ray. Thank you for your service.

— A. A.

Text Copyright © 2012 by Valerie Pfundstein
Illustration Copyright © 2012 by Aaron Anderson

Published in the United States by Pfun-omenal Stories, LLC. Deer Park, New York

Printed in the United States of America by Phoenix Color

10 9 8 7 6 5

Second edition, 2013

First edition published in 2012 by Novanglus Publishimg, LLC.

ISBN 978-0-578-13510-6 (HC)
ISBN 978-0-9906494-1-0 (PB)
LCCN 2012943227

Books are available in quantity for premium or promotional use.

Foreword

Veterans: Heroes in Our Neighborhood makes us more aware and appreciative of our everyday surroundings. Though most veterans rarely acknowledge their military service, this book reveals these brave people who live and work among us. When author Valerie Pfundstein—who lives nearby with her family and whose husband, a firefighter in the engine company at the same firehouse at which I was captain—told me she was inspired to honor family, neighbors, and friends who are veterans, I knew it was also a crucial opportunity to teach the next generation what it means to serve our country. The people commemorated in this book did, some of them having made the ultimate sacrifice so others could live free.

JOHN VIGIANO, SR.

United States Marine Corps, 1957–1962/1963–1966
Captain, Fire Department of New York, 1962–1998

John Vigiano, Sr., is an advocate on the Honorary Council for Hope For The Warriors®, a national nonprofit organization that stands together with and supports wounded U.S. service members, their families, and families of the fallen. Like the service men and women celebrated in this book, Mr. Vigiano heroically and humbly served America as a marine and his neighborhood as a captain in the New York Fire Department. Both of Mr. Vigiano's sons, John, Jr., a New York City firefighter and Joe, a New York City police detective, made the ultimate sacrifice in the attacks on the World Trade Center on September 11, 2001.

About the Author

Valerie Pfundstein has been a teacher, Girl Scout Leader, and advisor for a Boy Scout Venturing Crew. She is extremely grateful to the brave service men and women who protect our freedoms as Americans. She lives with her husband, Paul (a New York City Firefighter) and their three children on Long Island, New York. Valerie travels to schools throughout the country, speaking with students and encouraging them to write stories about their own veteran heroes. Veterans: Heroes in Our Neighborhood is her first book. Valerie has also written Mom's Choice Gold Award Winner - Lucky Him: He's the Fireman.

www.PfunomenalStories.com

Today we learned about our heroes,
a really special kind,
the ones who serve America
and leave their homes behind.

We read about the veterans
who give all they can give
to keep our country safe and free
so we can love and live.

Our teacher asked us each to name
a veteran we knew.
She said, "Now you may be surprised.
It won't be hard to do."

So after school
I asked my dad.
He had amazing news.
These heroes live
right in our town,
so many, who can choose?

They're our family, neighbors, friends,
who never boast or brag.
We all should be reminded of
their love for home and flag.

The man in town who cuts our hair
is known as Frank the barber,

but not too many know he was
a sailor at Pearl Harbor.

The butcher at the grocery store
who cuts the meat for stew
was once a paratrooper. Wow!

Matt served in World War II.

And Walter is a Navy man
who came to fix our heat.
He once fixed boilers on the ships

that sailed with the U.S. Fleet!

ARMY INFIRMARY

Our neighbor Jacqueline is a nurse
who wears a uniform.
She cared for wounded soldiers when
she served in Desert Storm.

Ernie is a firefighter.
We knew that he was brave!

And yet we never knew about
the Air Force time he gave.

And Edna, our librarian,
had a son named Jon.
He died while training for Iraq.
Now she's a Gold Star Mom.

Our mailman is a volunteer
who trains each year to serve.

When duty calls, Bob goes abroad.
He's in the Army Reserve.

And Manny is a proud Marine
who did a corporal's part.
He was wounded overseas
and wears a Purple Heart.

We celebrate our Veterans Day
the 11th of November.
We show our patriotic pride
and promise to remember.

Our heroes' headstones wear the flag
from coast to coast in May.
It's how we honor those we've lost
and mark Memorial Day.

World War II
1944

Korean War
1950

Son
Iraq War

Afghanistan
2010

Iraq War
2004

We painted posters of our heroes
and marched in a parade

to thank these men and women for
their sacrifices made.

But we don't need a calendar
to celebrate the brave.
We pledge allegiance to the flag
and let those colors wave!

It doesn't matter
where they served,
what service branch
or rank.
What matters is
remembering them
and offering
our thanks!

FRANK FALOTICO
1908–1983

Mailman, 3rd Class
U.S. Navy Reserve (1944–1946)

WWII

Victory Medal
American Campaign Medal
Asiatic Pacific Campaign Medal
Navy Occupation Service Medal

My neighborhood hero
was a U.S. Postal worker.

EDNA COBY
1921–

Hospitalman, 2nd Class
U.S. Navy, WAVES (1944-1946)

WWII

Gold Star Mom

My neighborhood hero
is an Episcopal Church volunteer.
At 90, she still works as an office
and warehouse assistant.

JACQUELINE A. GORDON
1964–

Lieutenant Colonel
U.S. Army Reserve (1984–present)

Desert Storm (Germany)
Guantanamo Bay (Cuba)
Iraq (Baghdad)

Army Commendation Medal

My neighborhood hero
is a school guidance counselor.

JONATHAN COBY
1961–1984

2nd Lieutenant
U.S. Army (1982–1984)

Died in a helicopter accident
during military training at the
age of 23.